It's April Fools' Day at the North Pole
©2021 Deborah Knopf

All rights reserved. This book or any portion thereof may not be reproduced or used in any manner whatsoever without the express written permission of the publisher except for the use of brief quotations in a book review.

ISBN: 979-8-9856536-2-5

Printed in the USA
Signature Book Printing, www.sbpbooks.com

Yay, it's April Fools' Day
Here at the great North Pole
With a whole day of pranks
Played by the young and the old

The elves are so excited
That this day is finally here
Because today, just like Christmas
Only comes once a year

A full day of fun
You can only imagine
It's a day like no other
Because anything can happen!

The elves are quite hungry
For their first meal of the day
But little do they know
Mrs. Claus plays the first trick today

She usually prepares goodies galore
But what do they see instead?
A table full of corn and broccoli
And brussels sprouts for breakfast!

"Oh, that was a good one"
The elves say while grinning
"But just you wait and see
All Fools' Day is just beginning!"

Mrs. Claus gives a chuckle
And brings pancakes to the table
When Finn and Jingle finish eating
They head out to the stable

Upon opening the stable door
What did they find in there?
Not one single reindeer
But a barn full of polar bears!

They say, "The joke's on us"
Because they both well knew
That Logan, Max and Cookie
Pulled off the old switcheroo!

Now we see Pixie and Trixie
Are a mischief making pair
Because the trick they play today
Is one that leads to a scare

Can you imagine the commotion
While they are pulling this prank?
They ran around shouting...
"Frosty fell in the hot tub and shrank!"

Scout is known as "the trickster"
He has a clever head
So there's really no surprise
When he plays this trick on Fred

The elves all know
That Fred has no clue
When they smother him with affection
Fred doesn't know what to do

Scout put this note on Fred's back...
"I'm having a really rough day
Please be a pal and give me a hug
And tell me everything will be okay!"

Here, Chloe asks Merry
To join her in a prank
And being such a fun-loving elf
She would never say, "No thanks!"

So they hurry out to the garden
And Chloe then explains
That they will do some digging
And remove all the candy canes

Then when Sprinkles arrives
To gather up these treats
Much to her surprise
She'll be pulling up BEETS!

With Rudolph as their guide
The reindeer go out to fly
To practice all their tricks
High up in the sky

After their training is over
And reaching their daily goal
They land and see a sign which reads
"Welcome to the great SOUTH POLE!"

Rudolph suddenly gasps and thinks
"Oh no, have we flown far astray?"
But just then he remembers
"Ah, it's just April Fools' Day"

Being such a thoughtful elf
Joy hands out a healthy snack
And gives some juicy apples
To Charlie, Nick and Jack

Jack decides to take the first bite
Then notices something that squirms
But after getting a closer look
He sees they're just gummy worms!

Outside, Rudolph is smiling
Is he going to trick someone?
Santa and the elves aren't the only ones
Who will join in this day of fun!

Rudolph is watching Dash
Looking for Old Saint Nick
And chuckles when he hears him yell
"Santa, you must come quick!"

"I was running past the stable
And this news you will not like
No sir, it's the worst thing imaginable
The reindeer, they've gone on strike!"

Here is unsuspecting Walter
Almost finished reading his book
He's tempted to know the ending
But determined not to look

It's a great mystery novel
With lots of plots and twists
He's only a page away from knowing
Just who the culprit is!

His heart is beating faster
Is it the villain that everyone feared?
But when Walter goes to turn the page
He sees the last page has disappeared!

Oh, but hiding in this room
Is a smirking, impish elf
Who has removed this last page
And is holding it himself!

Eve and Noelle are best of sisters
So it's really no surprise
That they brilliantly collaborated
To come up with this disguise

They would have to time it perfectly
Because everyone is on the lookout
But no one expected this to happen
During today's afternoon cookout

When the girls sat down at the table
Eve was covered in red spots
Causing all the elves to scatter and yell
"Oh no, Eve has the chicken pox!"

Here we see sneaky Shawn
Hiding behind the pine tree
You know, most elves have no idea
He's friends with a unicorn of the sea!

So, Shawn asked this friend for a favor
To help him this afternoon
Would she surprise Rudy and Sam
When they go out fishing in the lagoon?

At precisely half past one
On the ice, having a great time
Rudy begins to yell really loud
"Something big has bit my line!"

"Sam, we caught the big one
This fish is a monster
Help me keep her on the pole
We sure don't want to lose her!"

After struggling for an hour
Can you imagine their startle?
When Rudy reels in this big one
And sees it's Nora the Narwhal?

It's no secret to the elves
On the first day of the month
Santa conducts his chimney practice
Two hours after eating his lunch

They planned far ahead
So when the clock struck "two"
Santa then touched his nose
And up the chimney he flew

Oh, but Santa was surprised
The moment he got up inside
"The elves really got me this time"
With a smile Santa could not hide

They stuffed the chimney with balloons
And now seeing Santa was stuck
The elves were glad for his sense of humor
And that Santa was not "claus-trophobic"!

The elves just left to go skiing
Of this, Santa is aware
So fooling them after their chimney stunt
Yes, that would only be fair!

Later, as the elves return
Santa sees their faces turn pale
When they see the sign that he posted...
The North Pole is now "FOR SALE"!

During dinner, the elves all chat
About everyone being so clever
Then the elves all agree
That this was the best day ever!

At the end of the evening
When it's time to hit the hay
They immediately begin plotting
For next year's April Fools' Day!